KING KONG

by Ian Thorne

Reprinted 1982

Library of Congress Catalog Card Number: 76-051147.

International Standard Book Numbers:
0-913940-69-0 Library Bound
0-913940-76-3 Paperback

Design - Doris Woods and Randal M. Heise.

PHOTOGRAPHIC CREDITS:

Forrest J. Ackerman: from RKO Radio Pictures — 2, 8-9, 11, 12, 18, 19, 21, 22-23, 25, 27, 28, 31
Vincent Miranda, Jr.: from RKO — 13, 14, 15, 16, 17, 26, 29, 32, 33, 34: from Toho — 35, 38; from 20th Century Fox — 40-41
Paramount Pictures Corp.: Cover, 6, 43, 44-45, 46, 47
Toho Studios: 36

KING KONG

THE GREAT APE

The creature that walked like a man, but was not a man. A beast that was so big, it could pick up people as if they were toys. The huge black monster that killed . . .

All of these nightmares came to life in King Kong. At the beginning of the movie, the audience was told!

"You are going to see a story about Beauty and the Beast." Then an old Arab proverb was quoted: "And lo! The Beast looked upon the face of Beauty. And it stayed its hand from killing. And from that day, it was as one dead."

The story began with Carl Denham. He was a daredevil movie-maker of the 1930's. He would go to faraway places: jungles, high mountains, and dangerous deserts, to make thrilling movies.

Now he was on the track of the biggest thrill of all.

Denham had a map. It showed a mysterious island. The island was supposed to be the home of a Malay devil-god named Kong.

Denham went to the captain of a ship, Wanderer. "Captain Englehorn," he said, "I want to hire you and your ship to take me to Skull Island. I want to find Kong and make a movie about him.

An actors' agent (right) tells Carl Denham that no young actress wants to go on a crazy expedition to search for a giant ape. Denham is played by Robert Armstrong. In the center are Captain Englehorn (Frank Reicher) and first mate Jack Driscoll (Bruce Cabot).

The captain smiled. He thought Denham was a bit crazy. However, his money was good! "All right, we'll help you look for your island. When we find it, we'll help you make a movie of your monster. If he's there!"

Denham wanted a large crew. He would need help. He filled the ship with guns and explosives. But before he set sail, he needed one more thing — a beautiful girl.

"I don't want to haul a girl around," Denham told a newspaper reporter. "But movie fans expect it."

Denham had a strange way of getting a young

woman for his movie. He went ashore and just began looking around. It was the time of the Great Depression. Millions of people were out of work and very poor.

Denham heard a scream. He was passing a fruit stand. The owner had discovered a hungry young woman trying to steal an apple. She was lovely.

"How would you like a job?" Denham asked. "I can offer you money, fame, the thrill of a lifetime, and a long sea voyage that starts at six tomorrow morning."

Ann Darrow, broke and starving, agreed to come.

The Wanderer sailed for Skull Island. During the voyage, Denham taught Ann Darrow how to act in his movie. All she had to do was look scared!

Ann became friendly with the ship's first mate. He was a handsome young man named Jack Driscoll. Jack let Ann play with his pet monkey. When Denham saw lovely Ann and the ugly monkey, he said:

"Beauty and the Beast, eh? That's the idea for my picture! The Beast was a tough guy. He could lick the world. When he saw Beauty, the Beast went soft. He forgot his wisdom . . . and the little guys got him."

The ship arrived at the mysterious island. Denham led heavily-armed crewmen ashore. They heard natives chanting.

They came upon the island people getting ready to make a sacrifice to Kong! The natives were in front of a huge wall. Behind a large, heavy door in the wall, Kong waited for his victim.

The native chief had planned to sacrifice one of the village girls. Then he saw Ann! He offered to trade six island girls to Denham for the Golden Woman. Ann would be a perfect victim for Kong!

Of course Denham refused the trade. The natives became very angry. The would-be movie-makers had to flee back to the ship.

"But we'll be back tomorrow!" Denham shouted.

The island people decide that golden-haired Ann Darrow (Fay Wray) would make a perfect sacrifice to Kong.

Men from the island snatch Ann from the ship.

That night, Jack Driscoll and Ann stood on deck under the stars.

"Denham must be mad, putting you in a spot like that. You're not going back there," Jack said.

"I must," Ann said. "He has done so much for me."

"But if anything happened to you —" Jack said. "I love you, Ann."

"I love you too, Jack," Ann said. But then came the voice of Captain Englehorn, calling Driscoll. Ann said she would wait for him.

Ann gazed at the stars. They were very beautiful. If only the drums would stop beating! They made her very afraid.

Ann dreamed of romance. But as she stood on deck, hands reached out for her! Men from the village had paddled out to the ship. They grabbed Ann and dragged her away.

The village witch-doctor chained Ann to Kong's altar. It was like some terrible dream! Ann was in a trance as the great gate closed, leaving her alone in Kong's world beyond the wall.

Then Kong came and Ann screamed.

Ann is taken to the place of sacrifice.

Denham, Driscoll, and the ship's crew go into a swamp of monsters as they try to rescue Ann.

Back on the ship, Driscoll and Denham heard her cry out. They rushed to shore with a group of armed sailors.

"Open the gate!" Jack ordered. His men obeyed. They were just in time to see a huge form disappear into the jungle, carrying Ann.

Jack cursed Denham. It was all his fault! Quickly, he decided they would have to give chase. Englehorn and part of the crew stayed to keep the gate open. Jack, Denham, and the others ran into the Skull Island wilderness after Kong.

There were other monsters on the island besides Kong.

Dinosaurs attacked the men. Bullets had no effect on the creatures, so Driscoll drove them off with gas bombs. More and more dinosaurs came! Crewmen died horribly in the jaws of the monsters.

The men tried to escape one dinosaur by crossing a log that bridged a deep ditch. Then they saw Kong! The huge ape, 50 feet tall, grabbed one end of the log and shook the men off like dolls. Jack Driscoll and Denham escaped with their lives, but the other men died in the fall.

Kong shakes his pursuers into a deep ravine.

A tyrannosaurus attacked the mighty Kong himself. The great ape placed Ann in the top of a tree. There she watched as Kong battled the dinosaur to the death.

Kong then took his prize and carried her off. During all of the action, Kong had been very careful not to hurt Ann Darrow. She belonged to him. He liked the tiny, blonde creature that lay screaming in his huge paw.

Kong climbed to his lair high in the mountains of Skull Island. He took Ann with him. Unknown to the monster, Jack Driscoll followed.

As Kong gazed at the frightened girl, there was a strange cry. A giant flying lizard, a pterodactyl, swooped down toward Kong's ledge. The beast wanted Ann, too.

Kong gave a bellow of rage. His teeth flashed in anger. Would any other monster dare to take Ann away from him?

The pterodactyl flew at the ape. Kong was a match for the flapping horror. His mighty arms reached out and crushed the winged lizard.

During the battle, Jack reached the ledge where Ann lay. He took her to a long vine. The two of them began to slide down it toward the lake below.

Denham flings a gas bomb at Kong.

Kong saw them and began to pull in the vine! Ann and Jack tumbled down . . . down . . . and splashed into the saving waters of the lake. Ann and Jack fled to the great wall — with Kong following after them.

Captain Englehorn and Denham met them. The gate was barred; but Kong, on the rampage, broke it down. The great ape smashed the native village.

"Get the gas bombs!" Denham shouted, and finally Kong was conquered. He fell senseless on the beach.

"We'll take him back with us," Denham said. "The whole world will pay to see this! We will be millionaires."

And so Kong, wrapped in chains, was hauled into the ship and brought to New York.

Posters and a theater signboard proclaimed his coming!

KING KONG — 8TH WONDER OF THE WORLD!

As the people inside the theater waited, Denham came before the curtain. He told the onlookers about the captive from Skull Island and the curtain rose to show the 50-foot ape.

"Look at Kong!" Carl Denham said. "He was king and god in the world he knew. But he comes to civilization as a captive — a show to satisfy your curiosity. Now I want to introduce Ann Darrow, the bravest girl I have ever known."

Ann and Jack Driscoll stepped forward. Denham said: "There the Beast — and here the Beauty!"

Flashbulbs from hundreds of cameras began to go off all over the theater. Kong blinked, then roared. He began to struggle.

"He thinks we're attacking the girl," Denham cried.

The chains and hoops of steel that had held Kong began to break. The audience screamed as the huge beast began to break free. People started to run. Ann, Jack, and Denham fled into the wings of the stage.

And then Kong was free!

He bounded out into the streets of New York.

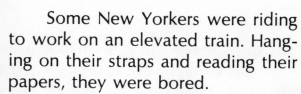

Some New Yorkers were riding to work on an elevated train. Hanging on their straps and reading their papers, they were bored.

Suddenly a face leered into the train's window! It was King Kong. He grabbed the train as if it were some serpent. He lifted it from the track and shook it. Tiny figures fell out, but none of them were Ann Darrow.

Kong went to look for her somewhere else.

Kong peered into the windows of huge buildings. He went stamping through the streets, spreading terror as he searched for the tiny blonde woman. In some strange way, the 50-foot giant was in love with Ann Darrow.

Meanwhile, Denham and the police were trying to think of a way to stop the monster. How do you destroy a 50-foot ape — without destroying New York, too?

Ann Darrow and Jack Driscoll waited inside a hotel while the search went on. Jack tried to comfort Ann. While they talked, a huge eye appeared at the window of the hotel room.

Ann screamed, and Kong knew that he had found his lost love. A huge, hairy paw reached into the room. The wall crumbled.

Gently, the fingers closed around Ann's body. Kong carried Ann away with him as Driscoll watched in helpless horror.

Where could Kong go? Skull Island was so far away. Kong was trapped in a modern city. It was an unfamiliar world. A world that was frightening — even to a 50-foot ape.

His island home had been in a high place, so Kong looked for the highest place he could find. He took Ann to the Empire State Building, the highest building in the world at that time. He climbed up its sides to the very top, carrying Ann with him.

"There's one thing we haven't thought of," Jack exclaimed. "Airplanes! If he should put Ann down, they could fly close enough to pick him off!"

25

A call went out to a nearby Air Corps training field. Within moments, biplane trainers were speeding over Manhattan, ready to battle the monster with their machine guns.

The monster gazed in surprise as the airplanes circled him. He decided they were enemies, like the pterodactyl on faraway Skull Island. They wanted his beautiful little woman! He would show them that he was still King Kong!

Carefully, the beast placed Ann on a ledge. As Kong prepared to do battle, Jack crept out to help Ann to safety.

Ann and Jack cower on the ledge.

The pilots saw that Ann was safe. They began the attack! Bullets poured out of machine guns, piercing Kong's thick hide.

He crushed one of the flying tormentors. But others dived on him. He lost his grip on the slippery skyscraper and fell down . . . down to the street below.

Ann, Jack, and Denham viewed the body of Kong. Ann could not help wiping away a tear. Jack said, "I know, you've just got something in your eye."

A policeman said: "Well, Denham, the airplanes got him."

"Oh, no," said the movie-maker, hands in his pockets. "It wasn't the airplanes. It was Beauty killed the Beast."

King Kong lies dead.

CHILDREN OF KONG

The movie King Kong opened in New York in 1933. It was a great success. Kong found a whole new world of fans when it was presented on television. The old film is still to be seen almost every year, both on TV and in theaters. Some people believe it still will be playing in 2001.

The man who was the "father" of Kong was Merian C. Cooper. He was a documentary film-maker with a fine sense of adventure, who had made movies in Iran and Siam. He wanted to do a film about living monsters such as African gorillas and the huge dragon-lizards of Komodo Island.

He presented his idea to RKO Pictures. The studio liked the idea, but decided to use models instead of living animals. By means of "stop-motion" photography, the models could be made to move and seem alive. One frame of film at a time was shot. The model was moved a tiny bit for each frame. When the frames were run quickly, the models looked alive.

Marcel Delgado was the model-maker who created Kong. Willis O'Brien was the special effects master who brought the monster to life.

King Kong, the great ape who terrified millions, was really a wire model covered with rabbit fur. He was only 18 inches tall.

Merian C. Cooper's pipe dream of a fabulous monster gave the movie world the immortal King Kong.

Six months after the success of King Kong, RKO released a sequel, Son of Kong.

Poor Carl Denham! He was going to make a million from Kong. Instead, he was sued by half the people in New York because of the damage the great ape did.

Denham fled civilization. He went back to Skull Island, taking with him a girl named Hilda, whom he loved.

Denham and Hilda discovered another ape! But the ape was much smaller than Kong, with white fur. The 12-foot "Kiko, son of Kong" was trapped in a pool of quicksand. When Denham and Hilda rescued him, he became their friend.

Denham and Hilda (Helen Mack) discover the son of Kong trapped in quicksand.

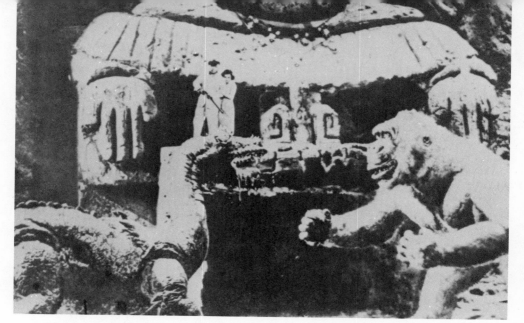

The young ape fights a dinosaur while Denham and Hilda hide on a ruined temple.

Denham came to Skull Island hoping to find a treasure which would restore his lost fortunes. Fighting off dinosaurs on the way, the white ape led Denham and Hilda to the gold.

Later the treasure hunters were threatened by a crook named Hellstrom, who had killed Hilda's father years before. Hellstrom was finally killed when the volcanoes of Skull Island erupted. Denham, Hilda, and the faithful crew members fled. Once when it seemed that Denham would drown, the Son of Kong held him above the waves until rescuers arrived. Denham was saved, but they could not save the white ape, who sank slowly beneath the sea.

"Poor little Kong," said Denham. "Do you think he knew he was saving my life?"

The question was unanswered. With the gold and Hilda, Carl Denham sailed back to civilization and ended the movie.

The first of the Kong look-alikes was Mighty Joe Young. This interesting 1949 movie used special effects by Kong creator Willis O'Brien, who won an Oscar for them. It also was directed by the man who directed King Kong — Ernest V. Schoedsack.

Mighty Joe was a 12-foot gorilla. He was taken to New York from Africa to become a night club star. But civilization proved too much for him. He went on a rampage, and it was ordered that he be shot on sight.

Human friends tried to rescue Mighty Joe. In the end, Joe saves children from a burning orphanage and is forgiven for his crimes.

In a happy ending, he goes back to Africa, together with his friends.

Mighty Joe, clutching a child, attempts a fiery rescue.

34

Mighty Joe Young was played for laughs.

An attempt to re-create the terror of Kong took place in 1960. Konga was the story of a mad scientist who used a secret serum to turn a mild chimpanzee into an ever-growing giant ape. Carrying the scientist in his paw, Konga stalked through London.

Instead of stop-motion photography, this movie used a cheaper plan. An actor, dressed in a gorilla suit, was made to seem huge by special effects.

By the 1960's, a new kind of monster movie had been born. The Japanese film studio, Toho, began producing full-color movies starring a prehistoric monster with radioactive breath, named Godzilla.

Godzilla was popular not only in Japan, but in the United States, too. Among the many sequels to the original movie was King Kong Versus Godzilla. It was produced in 1963.

This entertaining movie was aimed at young children, and they loved it! The monsters were funny and lovable, as well as destructive.

King Kong seemed to have grown to at least twice his former size as he fought with Godzilla. The clever Japanese made two endings for the movie. In the Japanese version, Godzilla won the big fight. In the American version, King Kong was the winner.

Everyone knew that neither monster was really dead. People waited eagerly for a sequel.

The meeting of the monsters! King Kong vs. Godzilla!

King Kong is kidnapped.

King Kong Escapes (1967) had a lot of funny moments. The great ape was captured by an evil scientist who intended to conquer the world. He was taken to the mountains by a fleet of helicopters, hypnotized, and forced to dig radioactive minerals.

The radioactivity broke the hypnotic spell, and King Kong escaped! He fled and turned up in Japan. The evil scientist brought a robot Kong, to capture the real ape. The climax of the movie has furry Kong fighting robot Kong while the fate of the world hangs in the balance.

Charleton Heston rides the hard way in **Planet of the Apes.**

There have been other ape monster movies besides those based on King Kong. Edgar Allan Poe's Murders in the Rue Morgue, the story of a killer-ape, has been filmed twice. The 1940's movies that were made at a lower cost included failures like Bela Lugosi's Ape Man, and Return of the Ape Man. In those films, the great Dracula had to act the role of a part-ape, part-werewolf like monster.

A far better group of movies was Planet of the Apes. In the original film, astronauts crash on a planet ruled by intelligent apes. The planet turns out to be the Earth in the distant future, when man has become animal-like, and the apes civilized.

Very good "makeup men" changed human actors into believable apes in Planet, which was a great hit in 1968. Beneath the Planet of the Apes followed in 1970. In it, another astronaut comes to the planet. He discovers an underground race of strange mole-like people who fight with the apes for mastery of the world.

Escape from the Planet of the Apes (1971) saw three intelligent apes go back in time to modern day Earth. They were considered a problem to humans. Even though they were innocent, they had to flee from the government killers.

Two other movies, Conquest of the Planet of the Apes (1972) and Battle for the Planet of the Apes (1974) continued the story. There was also a short-lived TV series based on the movies.

Meanwhile, the original King Kong was still popular. Every time it was shown on TV, millions watched. Movie producers of the 1970's began to plan not just one but two remakes of the original Kong.

For one thing, they thought it would be exciting to see the giant ape in color. For another, they wanted to include more violence than had taken place in the original movie. In the beginning, the 1933 version of Kong included scenes showing Kong eating people and committing other bloody acts. These scenes were cut out by the censor. It was thought such horrors should not appear in a movie that would be seen by young people.

All that had changed by the 1970's. By then, movies had ratings. Parents could tell by checking the rating whether the movie was suitable for young children. Older people were not especially scared by scenes of gory killings any more.

King Kong was brought back to life after 43 years! Italian producer Dino de Laurentiis made a modern day movie of King Kong, released in 1976. Another studio planned to re-create the old time Kong by setting their new film in the 1930's.

The 1976 version of **King Kong** *updated the old story.*

The de Laurentiis movie cost 24 million dollars to make. The title role went to a 47-foot mechanical ape. He was made to move by 20 technicians, who worked an electronic control board. The stop-motion Kong of 1933 had moved with a slightly jerky effect. New style machines gave the ape-monster a smoother, more life-like motion. The modern ape machine was the reason for the high cost of the movie.

Jessica Lange doesn't realize that Kong wants to be friends.

The mechanical monster was used mostly in close-ups. For long shots, such as Kong in his jungle home and Kong destroying New York, de Laurentiis used a man in a gorilla suit. Carefully detailed miniature buildings were built. The 6-foot ape seemed to be 40 feet tall when he rampaged among them, stomping them to bits.

The plot of the new King Kong is very much like that of the old. Only the people are changed to make them modern. The hero is a scientist instead of the first mate of a tramp steamer. The heroine is a hip, wise-cracking movie starlet. She treats the love-sick giant ape with dry humor instead of spending her time screaming, as the Ann Darrow of 1933 did.

The mighty Kong once again becomes a very sad sideshow freak. Once again, he breaks free and is hunted down. Even the airplane scene is re-created, and this time with helicopters.

The ending must always be the same. Beauty destroys the Beast. King Kong topples from the tower of the World Trade Center and dies.

Jessica Lange and Jeff Bridges stand sorrowfully beside the body of poor Kong.

Along with the heroine, we cannot help but shed a tear. Poor giant ape, the little guys always get him in the end.